Joel Smith worked as a journalist before moving into the community development and education sector where he has worked for ten years. He is now supervisor of the North Leitrim Men's Group community employment scheme where he works with men to improve their personal, social and technical skills. He has also trained as an IT and literacy tutor.

About Diffusion books

Diffusion publishes books for adults who are emerging readers. There are two series:

 Books in the Diamond series are ideally suited to those who are relatively new to reading or who have not practised their reading skills for some time (approximately Entry Level 2 to 3 in adult literacy levels).

 Books in the Star series are for those who are ready for the next step. These books will help to build confidence and inspire readers to tackle longer books (approximately Entry Level 3 to Level 1 in adult literacy levels).

Other books available in the Diamond series are:

Space Ark by Rob Childs

Snake by Matt Dickinson

Fans by Niall Griffiths

Breaking the Chain by Darren Richards

Uprising by Alex Wheatle

Other books available in the Star series are:

Lost at Sea

Joel Smith

diffusion

First published in Great Britain in 2017

Diffusion
an imprint of SPCK
36 Causton Street
London SW1P 4ST
www.spck.org.uk

ISBN 978-1-908713-09-4
eBook ISBN 978-1-908713-20-9

Typeset by Manila Typesetting Company
Printed in Great Britain by Ashford Colour Press
Subsequently digitally reprinted in Great Britain

eBook by Manila Typesetting Company

Produced on paper from sustainable forests

Contents

Contents

1
Off to sea

Alec Compton was in the Royal Navy. He was at the port ready to sail off on a new mission. He just needed to say goodbye to his mum first.

'You have always made me proud of you,' said Alec's mum. 'So do your best, just like always.'

'Of course I will,' Alec said.

He looked at his mother and saw the worry lines on her forehead and the grey colour of her skin.

'How are you feeling now?' asked Alec.

'OK,' she replied.

'Go home,' Alec told her. 'Don't wait around to see me off. It's too cold. And don't forget to go to the doctor today, like I said.'

'All right,' she said. 'Lucky old you, going to the Mediterranean for some sun!'

His mum said she would not wait around in the cold, but Alec knew she would. She would not leave before the ship sailed. She loved him so much that she would want to wave him off.

They hugged each other one last time. Then Alec walked up the narrow gangway on to the ship.

At the top of the gangway, he saluted his boss. Then he said hello to his friends Max and Bill.

Max could tell that Alec was not as cheerful as usual. Something was wrong.

'What's wrong? Didn't your girlfriend come to see you off?' Max asked, laughing.

'There is more to life than girlfriends, you know,' said Alec.

'That's not like you. What's wrong?' asked Max again.

'I'm worried about my mum,' said Alec. 'She doesn't look well.'

'Did you tell her to go to the doctor?' asked Max.

'Yes,' replied Alec, 'but I don't know if she will listen.'

'Of course she will,' said Max.

Alec waved a final goodbye to his mum. Then he went below deck. Alec had not been on the ship for a while. He had to remember to keep his head down. He was tall and the ceiling was low.

He found his cabin, which he would share with eight other men. There were three bunk beds, each with three beds one on top of the other. The bunks were very close together and there was not much room to move about. He hoped that there would be no one who snored loudly in the cabin. He was a very light sleeper.

After he had put away his bags, Alec went up to the bridge of the ship. This was where the ship was steered from.

Alec's job in the Royal Navy was as a 'Seaman Specialist'. This meant he had to help steer the ship out of port. He also helped to rescue stranded boats. It was an exciting job and Alec loved it.

Alec had a fantastic view from the ship's bridge. It was a cold day, but the sun was shining. The ship, the *HMS Glory*, was huge.

It had a crew of three hundred and fifty people and was about the size of one and a half football pitches. It made all the other boats in the harbour look tiny.

Two tug boats helped to take the ship out of port. Alec watched the screen and steered the course that had been set.

What do you think?

- What is Alec's job? Why do you think he enjoys it so much?

- How do you think Alec felt when he said goodbye to his mum? How do you think his mum felt?

- What do you think it would be like to share a small room with eight other people? What could you do, or not do, to make it easier?

2

Bad news

The next day, when his shift was over, Alec joined his friends for something to eat. The food was good on board ship. Tonight was Alec's favourite: fish and chips with mushy peas.

Alec sat down beside Max and Bill. The guys at the table were talking about their mission. Their job was to save lives. Lots of people were travelling to Europe in unsafe boats. The boats were too small to travel on the open sea and there were too many people on board them.

Sometimes they sank, and many people had drowned. The *HMS Glory* would look for these small boats and then take the passengers on board.

'Where are all these people coming from?' Max asked.

'All over Africa and the Middle East,' replied Bill, 'but mostly from Syria and Libya.'

'Why don't they stay where they are?' said Max. 'We have enough people in Europe already!'

'Don't be silly,' said Bill. 'Do you think they want to leave their homes and families to come to Europe? They have to leave. War has destroyed their homes and schools and hospitals.'

'Well, I don't see why we have to save the silly beggars,' said Max. 'We don't even have enough jobs for our own people. We can't take everyone in.'

'What do you think?' said Bill to Alec. 'You're very quiet.'

'To be honest, I couldn't care less about them,' Alec replied. He was thinking about his mum.

It wasn't easy to keep in touch with home. Every sailor was only allowed to call home for thirty minutes each week. They had to use a special Royal Navy phone. Usually Alec saved up his phone time to use all in one go, but he wanted to check whether his mum had gone to the doctor. He decided he could not wait. He would phone home today.

'Hello,' said Alec when he heard his mum's voice on the phone. 'It's me.'

'Hello, son,' she replied. Her voice sounded a bit shaky.

'Did you go to the doctor? Is everything all right?' Alec asked.

'Yes, everything is fine. I just have to go for a few scans,' said his mum. 'Why don't you talk to your sister? Here she is.'

Alec's sister, Jane, came on the phone.

'What's wrong with Mum?' Alec asked her.

'The doctor thinks Mum might have cancer. He's found a lump,' said Jane. She sounded close to tears as she spoke.

'Can they do anything about it?' asked Alec.

'The doctor doesn't know,' replied Jane. 'They have to do more tests. We won't know anything for a few more days.'

Alec said goodbye and hung up the phone. He went to his bunk. He tried to read, but he kept thinking about his mum. He loved the Royal Navy but for the first time ever he wished he had another job. He wished he was closer to home.

He wanted to be there with his mum. He was stuck here in the middle of the ocean, and there was nothing he could do about it.

What do you think?

- What does Bill think about the refugees coming to Europe? What does Max think?

- What do you think about the refugees coming to Europe?

- What bad news does Jane give Alec? Why do you think his mum didn't tell him herself?

- Have you ever been away from home when there was bad news? Or good news? How did you feel?

3
Trouble

Over the next three days the weather got warmer. The ship sailed past France, Spain and Portugal and through the straits of Gibraltar into the Mediterranean Sea.

Alec, Max and Bill had finished their lunch but were still sitting at the table. They were talking about the good times they had spent together in Gibraltar.

Bill was reminding Alec about a time when he was nearly arrested outside a pub in Gibraltar.

'You were giving that cop a lot of cheek,'
said Bill.

'Yeah!' said Max. 'You were trying to steal his
helmet when that wild monkey came along and
did it for you!'

Alec, Max and Bill all laughed.

But it wasn't long before Alec was staring sadly
at the sea again.

'Come on! Don't be such a sad sack,' said Bill.

'Sorry. I can't help it,' said Alec.

'What's the matter? More bad news from home?'
asked Max.

'It's Mum,' explained Alec. 'I spoke to her again
this morning. She's going to have more tests at
the end of the week.'

Suddenly an officer, Commander Peters, came up to them.

'You three men,' he yelled, 'what do you think this is? A picnic? There's work to be done! In two days we will be picking up refugees from the eastern Mediterranean.'

He turned and said to Alec, 'I want you to check that the landing craft is in working order.'

But Alec was still thinking about his mum. He wanted to be left in peace. He didn't get up.

'Well?' said Commander Peters. 'What are you waiting for?'

'Whatever,' said Alec, as he slowly stood up.

Commander Peters did not like that. 'Don't speak like that to me!' he said angrily.

Alec pulled himself together. He saluted the officer.

'Come to my office straight away,' Commander Peters ordered him. Then he turned to Max and Bill. 'Back to work, you two, or you will be peeling potatoes for the rest of the mission!'

Alec didn't like to be in trouble. He was never in trouble, except for the odd night when he drank too much.

They reached the office. Commander Peters spoke to Alec.

'I've known you for three years,' he said, 'and you've never behaved so rudely. What's the matter?'

'Well, sir,' said Alec. 'It's my mum. She's ill.'

'How ill is she?' asked Commander Peters.

'She's going to have some tests at the end of the week. They think she has cancer,' replied Alec.

Commander Peters thought about this. Then he said, 'Almost every family has someone who has cancer. Doctors can do some amazing things now. I'm sure she will be all right.'

'Yes, sir,' said Alec. 'I hope so.'

'Let me know what happens,' said Commander Peters. 'If your mother gets worse, I'll see if I can arrange for you to have some time off. But the best thing for you to do now is keep busy. When we arrive, I want you to take charge of one of the landing craft. We will use them to pick up refugees. So go and check that everything is in good working order.'

'Thank you, sir,' said Alec.

Commander Peters' words made Alec feel better. He had always found it helpful to share his problems. But he still worried about his mum. What would the tests show?

What do you think?

- Why is Commander Peters angry with Alec? How does Alec feel about being in trouble?

- How do you feel if you're in trouble?

- Do you prefer to keep your problems to yourself or to share them? Who could you share your problems with?

- Can you think of some good ways to help reduce worrying?

4

In charge

Two days later, everyone swung into action. The ship's helicopters had spotted a refugee boat. Now the lookouts on board the ship could see it with their own eyes.

The *HMS Glory* had been designed so that landing craft could launch directly from inside the ship. There was a section in the bottom of the *HMS Glory* that took in water. When the ship's door opened, the landing craft just sailed out on to the sea.

Alec was in charge of one of the four landing craft. The sea was calm, but even so, the little boat bounced over the small waves. Alec loved the feeling of being in command of his own boat.

None of the men had been on a mission like this before. Nobody knew quite what to expect. Each of the four boats had eight sailors on board. They had to get the balance right. There had to be enough sailors to keep order. But they had to have enough space on the boat to rescue the refugees.

They soon reached the refugee boat. They could see that it was overloaded. It was an inflatable boat built for thirty people at most. There must have been a hundred and twenty people on board.

Bill was in charge of one of the other boats. He picked up a loudspeaker.

'OK,' he said. 'Everybody, keep calm.
We are going to take you off one at a time.
We don't want the boat to tip over.'

This was Alec's first chance to see the refugees.
They seemed to be mostly African or Arabic.
Some of them were shouting at him. He did not
like it. Just like Bill, he had a loudspeaker, but he
did not feel confident using it.

'All right, calm down!' shouted Alec. 'Calm down!
Just do as we say.'

The refugees seemed desperate. Some of them
shouted out for water. Other refugees shouted
out for food. Some refugees said nothing. Alec
thought they looked ill and weak. His crew
threw life jackets on to the refugee boat so
that the refugees would be safe even if they
fell into the sea.

Alec steered his boat along one side. Bill steered his boat along the other side.
The two other rescue boats waited behind Bill and Alec. Alec took his load of thirty people on board. Then he took his boat back to the ship.

Alec got off the boat and started to help the refugees out. He felt sorry for them, but he wondered what would happen if they all ended up in Britain. He didn't think the NHS could cope.

Suddenly he remembered his mum. How could the doctors treat her properly if they had so many refugees to look after?

What do you think?

- How does being in charge of his own boat and the other sailors make Alec feel?

- How would you feel about being put in charge of other people?

- How do you think Alec feels when he sees all the people in the boat? How do you imagine they feel when the Royal Navy arrives?

- Do you think the NHS could cope with all the people if they came to Britain?

5
A dangerous rescue

Alec and the other sailors spent two days rescuing people. The *HMS Glory* was in a mess. Everything was upside down. An extra five hundred refugees made the ship feel crowded. The refugees seemed to talk very loudly. It sounded like twenty different languages.

The doctors were worried about disease. The sailors had to wear masks if they went below deck.

At lunch on the third day, Max, Bill and Alec were having an argument.

'Look,' said Max, 'all I'm saying is that some of these people are from countries that are not at war.'

'Yes, but there must be big problems in their country if they are risking their lives to get to Europe,' replied Bill.

'OK, then, what about the Nigerians? They aren't at war,' said Max.

'What about them? I'm half Nigerian myself,' said Bill.

'Sorry! I didn't mean anything by it,' Max said.

Nobody spoke for a bit.

Max decided to change the subject. 'How is your mum?' he asked Alec. 'Have you heard anything else?'

'She had the tests,' Alec replied. 'We have to wait and see what the doctors say about the results.'

'Fingers crossed,' said Max.

Alec wished he was with his mum. Should he ask for some time off? He hated being so far away from her when she was ill.

His mum was always there when he needed her. She was always there when he was sick or got into trouble. Once he had got into a bad fight in school. His mum had stood by him. She made sure the school didn't kick him out. He made up his mind to ask for time off as soon as he could.

Suddenly, an officer came running in.

'You three!' he yelled. 'Get on to the boats now! It's an emergency. There's a boat out there full of people and it looks like a fire has started on board.'

This time, the sea was rough and it was a bit foggy. Alec was working on Bill's boat.

They could see that the refugee boat was in trouble. The fire wasn't big but it was pushing people to one side of the boat. Soon, the boat would tip over.

The *HMS Glory* shone its lights on the little boat to try to cut through the fog. The refugees held their hands over their eyes to cover them from the bright lights.

It looked like there were about eighty people on board. The boat was only built to take twenty people. The crew could hear the people shouting for help. Alec could hear a woman crying.

Alec and the rest of the crew were wearing gloves and masks. Alec thought it would look unfriendly to the refugees, but he knew he had to follow orders. There wasn't time to give out life jackets. They just had to start taking people on board.

It was very difficult in the rough water. Both boats were really bobbing up and down.
The fire had panicked everybody. Alec was giving the refugees a hand to get on board. There was a lot of shouting as the sailors tried to keep order.

Finally, there was just one woman left on the little boat. She seemed to have fainted. Alec and another sailor grabbed a stretcher and climbed on to the refugee boat. As they rolled the woman on to the stretcher they saw that she was pregnant.

It was very difficult to carry the woman. Alec was glad he was wearing a life jacket. The fire was getting bigger and they were feeling the heat. Alec knew they were in danger.
If the engine caught fire they would be in deep trouble.

Alec was still on the boat when – boom! The engine exploded.

What do you think?

- Why do Alec and the other sailors have to wear gloves and masks? How does it make Alec feel? How do you think it would make the refugees feel?

- What is the difference between a refugee and an economic migrant?

- Alec really misses his family and home. What are some good ways to cope with homesickness?

- Has anyone stood by you when you needed them to? Have you ever stood by anyone when they needed you to? How important is it to be there for each other?

6
Lost at sea

A wave splashed Alec's face and he woke up. He was in the sea! Cold, salty water was in his mouth and up his nose. 'What the hell happened?' he said.

His voice sounded funny. There was a buzzing in his ear. He reached up to his ear and felt blood. At the back of his head he could feel a bump. Something must have hit him on the back of the head. No wonder he had been knocked out.

Alec tightened the straps of the life jacket that had saved his life. As he did so he found that he was wearing gloves. He also felt a mask hanging from his head. He took the mask off and threw it away and kicked off his heavy boots.

Then he remembered. There had been an explosion on the refugee boat and he had been blown into the water. He hoped Bill and the other sailors were OK. He also hoped that the pregnant woman was safe.

Alec wasn't sure how long he had been knocked out for, but the fog was much thicker now. He slowly turned around, trying to catch sight of the *HMS Glory*, but he couldn't see anything.

He had done lots of 'man overboard' drills before, but this was the real thing. He knew that the crew of the *HMS Glory* would be looking for him and anyone else who had gone overboard.

Alec's ears were buzzing. He thought he could hear a helicopter, but he could not see it. His life jacket had a small light on it, but it would not be much help.

'Typical!' Alec said to himself. 'All the beautiful clear days in the Mediterranean, and I had to go overboard on a foggy day.'

He needed to stay awake so he tried to sing. It was a dirty song he had learned in Malta. He remembered the night he had learned it. He had met a lovely girl that night. He had written to her a few times, but the romance had fizzled out. If only he was in her arms now.

After a while Alec could no longer hear the helicopter. He started to worry that they might not find him after all. If he was not rescued soon he would die, not from drowning but because of the cold. He was getting really tired now.

Alec began to think about lots of things. He thought about his mother. She would be heartbroken if something happened to him. He hoped her test results would come back clear. Then he thought about his sister. She would look after Mum if he died.

If he got out of this alive he would leave the Royal Navy and find a job near home. He should be helping the people he loved, not out here risking his life for strangers.

Alec was feeling very unwell now. He was cold and his head ached. He felt sick. His arms and legs were too heavy to move. His body would not do what he asked it to.

By now he had lost all track of time. He shouted every now and again but he was giving up all hope of being rescued.

He could no longer keep his eyes open. He fell asleep but his dreams were unhappy.

What do you think?

- How does Alec feel when he is lost at sea? What is he thinking about?

- If you knew you only had a short time to live, who or what would you think about?

- What would you decide to do differently if you survived?

7

Rescued

When Alec woke up he was being pulled on to a little boat. It took three men to pull him out. He was too weak to help.

But it was not the Royal Navy that was rescuing him. He had been saved by refugees!

He was put down beside an African woman. His mouth and throat were dry. He tried to say 'water', but not much came out. The African woman seemed to understand that he was hungry and thirsty. She peeled a small orange.

She gave the orange to him. He closed his eyes as he ate it. Nothing had ever tasted so good. The woman was probably hungry and thirsty too, so it was kind of her to share what little she had.

By now the weather had cleared and the fog had gone.

Alec's body was slowly heating up but his head still hurt. He looked at the faces around him. The people looked as though they were from North Africa. They seemed happy to have saved him.

Maybe they have more chance of being rescued with me here, he thought. He hoped they were right. How strange that he had come over here to save them, but it was them who had saved him. He hoped that someone else would save them all now. He blacked out again.

When Alec woke the next time the little boat was in the shadow of a huge ship. Someone was throwing life jackets into their little boat. There was lots of shouting. The shouting sounded Italian. It was the Italian navy.

'We have been looking for you,' said one of the sailors to Alec in an Italian accent.

After a while someone pulled Alec off the refugee boat and on to the big ship. He was given an apple and a drink of water, like the rest of the refugees. He saw that the sailors wore masks and gloves. Now he understood how it felt for the refugees. He felt ashamed.

For a while, Alec was left sitting with the refugees. Then a doctor helped him to his feet. This doctor was not wearing a mask. Alec was taken to the medical room. The doctor checked him over and gave him some clean clothes.

Alec felt that the Italians were treating the refugees like animals compared to the way they were treating him.

Alec soon had some hot food inside him and a bandage around his head. He started to feel much better. His hearing still wasn't right, though.

An officer who spoke English came to see him. The officer said that Alec would be taken to the port of Brindisi in Italy. Someone from the Royal Navy would meet him there the next morning.

What do you think?

- Why do you think the refugees helped Alec?

- If you were hungry and thirsty, would you share the little bit of food you had?

- How is Alec treated differently from the refugees? Why is he treated differently? Is it fair?

8
Samira

Early the next morning Alec decided to go below deck. He wanted to try to find the men who had pulled him out of the water. He couldn't find them, but he did find the woman who had given him the orange.

He went straight up to her. 'Hello,' he said. 'You gave me an orange.'

'I know,' she said with a smile.

'I'm Alec. What's your name?' he asked.

'Samira,' she replied.

'Where are you from?' asked Alec.

'I am from South Sudan,' she replied.

'Do you have any family with you?' asked Alec.

She looked sad. 'No,' she said. 'My parents, brothers and sisters were killed in the civil war.'

'I'm sorry,' Alec said. 'What about your home?'

'It was burned to the ground,' she replied.

They were both silent for a moment. Alec was thinking how hard her life had been and how different it was from his own life. These people really did need help.

'Here is my address and phone number in England,' he said, 'in case you need some help.'

Samira gave him a big smile.

When they arrived at Brindisi in Italy, Alec was helped off the ship. It felt good to be on dry land.

A Royal Navy officer came to meet him. The officer welcomed him and took him to a smart black car with a driver from the embassy. He told Alec what was going to happen.

'We will travel by car to Rome,' he said. 'It will take about five hours, so try to get some sleep. When we get to Rome, a British doctor will check you over. Later today there will be a press conference with all the TV companies and newspapers at the embassy.'

The officer talked and talked. It was a while before Alec got a chance to say anything.

'Sir,' said Alec, 'please could I borrow your phone so that I can call my mum?'

'I'm sorry, I'm not allowed to let you talk to anyone yet,' replied the officer. 'Your family does know that you are safe.'

Alec felt cross, but there was no point arguing. Orders were orders. He sat in silence looking out of the tinted windows. There wasn't much to see. It was all motorways.

What do you think?

- How did Alec feel about the refugees at the beginning of the book? How does he feel about them now?

- Why do people leave the country they were born in for another country?

- Would you like to move to another country? Why, or why not?

- Why does Alec follow orders even when he doesn't like them? Is he right to do so? Could you?

9
Reunion

Alec had fallen asleep again. He couldn't seem to stay awake.

When he woke up, they were arriving in Rome. He had been dribbling against the window. He felt embarrassed. As they came to a stop, he wiped his mouth.

'You had better smarten yourself up,' said the officer. 'There are some journalists and photographers waiting for you. Don't say anything to them. They can wait until the press conference.'

As Alec got out of the car the journalists shouted questions to him. He walked past without saying anything.

Inside the embassy Alec felt the thick red carpet under his feet. He saw photographs of the Queen. The furniture looked very expensive, and the Queen's crown was printed on it.

'What a place,' Alec said to himself. 'Mum would love this.'

It was nice to be in such a posh place, but then he thought about Samira fleeing from hunger and war. What was happening to her now?

Alec was taken to a beautiful bedroom with its own bathroom. He showered, brushed his teeth and got dressed in a new uniform that had been laid out for him. He looked in the mirror at the bump on his head. It was going down slowly. He sat on the end of the bed, thinking.

He had thought that if he survived going overboard he would leave the navy. He wanted to be at home so that he could look after his mum. But now that he had met Samira he knew what an important job the Royal Navy did. People like her needed help. He was not sure what to do.

Then there was a knock on the door and a man came in.

'I'm Doctor Bhamjee,' he said. 'I've come to give you a check-up.'

'I thought I was going to see a British doctor,' said Alec.

'I am British! I'm from Brighton,' said Dr Bhamjee. 'My grandparents grew up in India. Then they moved to Brighton.'

'Sorry, I didn't mean anything by it,' said Alec.

'Don't worry,' said the doctor. 'I'm used to it.'

'Do you know much about cancer?' asked Alec as the doctor examined him.

'We can cure many cancers these days. Are you worried about a lump? Would you like me to check something for you?' asked Dr Bhamjee.

'No, it's not me, it's my mum,' said Alec. 'They think she has breast cancer.'

'They have very good success rates with breast cancer. My own wife had it,' said Dr Bhamjee, smiling.

'And is your wife OK?' Alec asked hopefully.

'I hope so. She's buying me dinner after this check-up!' said the doctor. 'How is your head?'

'It's not as bad as it was, but my hearing still isn't right,' answered Alec.

'Well, you will be flying home after the press conference. I'll order some tests for when you get there,' said Dr Bhamjee. 'I think it will take time for you to recover fully.'

The only word Alec heard was 'home'. It might not be easy if his mum was unwell, but he could not wait to see her and his sister.

What do you think?

- How does Alec feel about being in such a posh place as the embassy?

- Why didn't Alec think that the doctor was British? What makes a person British?

- Why does Alec want to leave the navy? Why does he want to stay?

- What could you do to help your family? What could you do to help strangers?

10
A surprise, or two

A press officer had told Alec that there would be a lot of journalists and photographers at the press conference. But he was not ready for all the sudden flashing cameras and clapping.

Alec sat between the press officer and the ambassador. There were journalists from the BBC, Sky, ITV and all the newspapers.

They asked Alec to explain what had happened. He told them that he and another sailor had tried to rescue a pregnant woman on a burning boat.

The boat had exploded and he had been thrown into the sea. He told them that he had been rescued by refugees. They had saved his life.

The press officer explained that the other sailor and the pregnant woman were safe too.

They asked Alec how he was feeling. He told them that he was fine except for a few bumps and bruises. And that he was a bit deaf in one ear.

'What does it feel like to be a hero?' asked one of the journalists.

Alec blushed. He had never thought of himself as a hero.

'I was just doing my job,' he told them.

'Do you think you will stay with the Royal Navy? Or will you go back home to a safe desk job?' asked another journalist.

Alec thought for a moment. He did not want to make up his mind in front of all these people.

Then Alec spoke. 'Well, to be honest, my mum isn't that well. If she gets worse, then I'll be happy to stay at home and look after her. I think I should talk to my family first.'

The press took some more photos of Alec, and then he was taken to a room with lots of books.

'Wait here, please,' said the ambassador. 'I'll be back in a moment.'

Alec wondered if something was wrong. Had he said the wrong thing to the press? He did not care. He had meant what he said about leaving the Royal Navy if his mum was unwell.

He saw that a table had been set for tea with three cups. He could not think who the cups would be for. Maybe more people from the press?

Then the door opened. Alec's mum and his sister came in. He could not believe it. He hugged them and cried. Alec's mum looked tired but happy.

'You shouldn't have come!' Alec said to his mum. 'But I'm so glad you did.'

'I wouldn't have missed it for the world,' she replied.

That night, they stayed at the embassy together. Alec had thought he might never see his family again. He felt lucky to be alive.

The Royal Navy gave Alec three months off so that he could recover and be with his mum.

At the end of three months, Alec was feeling back to normal. His mum was doing well too. She was having treatment for cancer. She had to give up the fags.

That made her a bit cranky at first,
but she was happy that the treatment
was working.

Alec had made up his mind to return to the Royal Navy. His hearing was almost perfect now. He had enjoyed his time off, and was happy that he had been there for his mum. But she was OK, and she wanted him out from under her feet!

He had packed his bags and was waiting for a taxi. Suddenly, he heard the doorbell ring. He grabbed his bags and opened the door. But it was not the taxi. It was a beautiful woman. She stood at the door, smiling at him. It was Samira, the woman from the refugee boat!

'Hi, Alec. It's me, Samira,' she said. 'Do you have time for a quick cup of coffee?'

He smiled at her.

'Well, not really. I've got a boat to catch,' said Alec. 'But I'll make time!'

What do you think?

- What makes a hero?

- Do you think Alec is a hero? Does he think of himself as a hero?

- Why do you think Samira has come to visit Alec?

- Would you like to join the navy, the army or the air force? Why, or why not?

Books available in the Diamond series

Space Ark
by Rob Childs (ISBN: 978 1 908713 11 7)
Ben and his family are walking in the woods when they are thrown to the ground by a dazzling light. Ben wakes up to find they have been abducted by aliens. Will Ben be able to defeat the aliens and save his family before it is too late?

Snake
by Matt Dickinson (ISBN: 978 1 908713 12 4)
Liam loves visiting the local pet shop and is desperate to have his own pet snake. Then one day, Mr Nash, the owner of the shop, just disappears. What has happened to Mr Nash? And how far will Liam go to get what he wants?

Fans
by Niall Griffiths (ISBN: 978 1 908713 13 1)
Jerry is excited about taking his young son Stevie to watch the big match. But when trouble breaks out between the fans, Jerry and Stevie can't escape the shouting, fighting and flying glass. And then Stevie gets lost in the crowd. What will Jerry do next? And what will happen to Stevie?

Breaking the Chain

by Darren Richards (ISBN: 978 1 908713 08 7)

Ken had a happy life. But then he found out a secret that changed everything. Now he is in prison for murder. Then Ken meets the new lad on the wing, Josh. Why does Ken tell Josh his secret? And could it be the key to their freedom?

Lost at Sea

by Joel Smith (ISBN: 978 1 908713 09 4)

Alec loves his job in the Royal Navy. His new mission is to save refugees from unsafe boats. But when a daring rescue attempt goes wrong, Alec is the one who needs saving. Who will come to help him?

Uprising: A true story

by Alex Wheatle (ISBN 978 1 908713 10 0)

Alex had a tough start in life. He grew up in care until he was fourteen, when he was sent to live in a hostel in Brixton. After being sent to prison for taking part in the Brixton riots, Alex's future seemed hopeless. But then something happened to change his life...

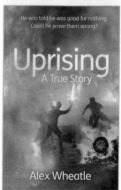

You can order these books by writing to Diffusion, SPCK, 36 Causton Street, London SW1P 4ST or visiting www.spck.org.uk/what-we-do/prison-fiction/